First published in Belgium and Holland by Clavis Uitgeverij, Hasselt – Amsterdam, 2015
Copyright © 2015, Clavis Uitgeverij

English translation from the Dutch by Clavis Publishing Inc. New York
Copyright © 2016 for the English language edition: Clavis Publishing Inc. New York

Visit us on the web at www.clavisbooks.com

Crocodile Is Hungry written and illustrated by Aurélia Higuet
Original title: *Krokodil heeft honger*
Translated from the Dutch by Clavis Publishing

ISBN 978-1-60537-264-8

This book was printed in January 2016 at Publikum d.o.o., Slavka Rodica 6, Belgrade, Serbia

First Edition
10 9 8 7 6 5 4 3 2 1

Aurélia Higuet

Crocodile
Is Hungry

Clavis

NEW YORK

Crocodile loves food.
And today he is **HUNGRY**!
What can he eat?

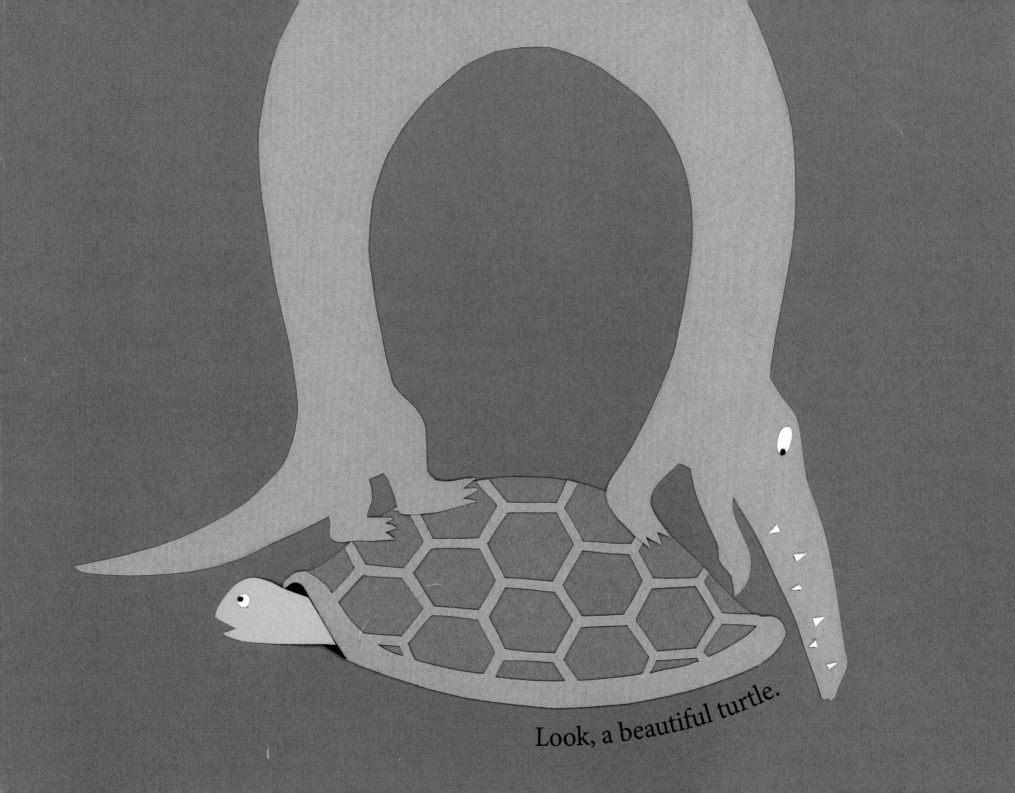

Look, a beautiful turtle.

Unfortunately it is too **HARD**.

And there is a cute little hedgehog.
But all those small spines
are so PRICKLY.

Hey, there's a rabbit….
But it is too **FAST**
to catch!

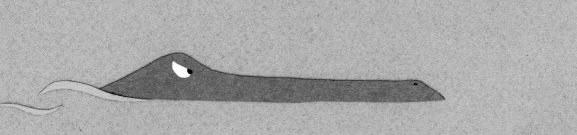

Maybe that little frog?
No, it **JUMPS** away
and disappears under water.

The giraffe might make a good meal,
but it is far
too **FRIENDLY**....

How about the chameleon?
No, it makes Crocodile
DIZZY.

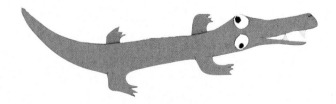

What about some honey?
Definitely not!
The bee is **PROTECTiNG** the beehive….

Maybe the little mouse?
No, it **HIDES** so well,
Crocodile can't see it in the tall grass.

"CAREFUL, LiTTLE BOY!"
all the animals shout
when Crocodile snaps at him.

But Crocodile is not in the mood
for a little boy.
He wants the juicy **RED APPLE!**
YUM!